HOMES Afloat

My sincere thanks to the following people for their time, information, images and enthusiasm for this book:

Professor Philip Crossley, Western State Colorado University, the USA

Sonya Law, Melbourne, Australia

Nancy Kelly, The Asia Foundation, San Francisco, the USA

Dear Reader

While researching this book, I found out about many interesting and varied cultures that have adapted to life on and around bodies of water. Part 1 is devoted to the Aztecs, who had one of the world's oldest and most ingenious "floating" agricultural systems. In Chapter 4, there's an easy chocolate drink for you to make, based on an Aztec recipe. In Part 2, go on a virtual voyage to other communities living and working on canals, rivers and lakes around the world.

> "A WONDER OF THE *CHINAMPAS* IS HOW THE AZTECS FARMED A WETLAND ENVIRONMENT PRODUCTIVELY AND SUSTAINABLY."
>
> PROFESSOR PHILIP CROSSLEY

It's not just people who live on or around water, of course. In Chapter 12, you will read about the plight of polar bears that hunt from floating sheets of sea ice. You'll find out about how their seasonal floating "homes" are melting earlier than usual as a result of changing climatic conditions in the Arctic region.

Sharon Parsons

Contents

HOMES Afloat

PART ONE: AN ANCIENT FLOATING EMPIRE

PART TWO: FLOATING COMMUNITIES

1 The Aztecs

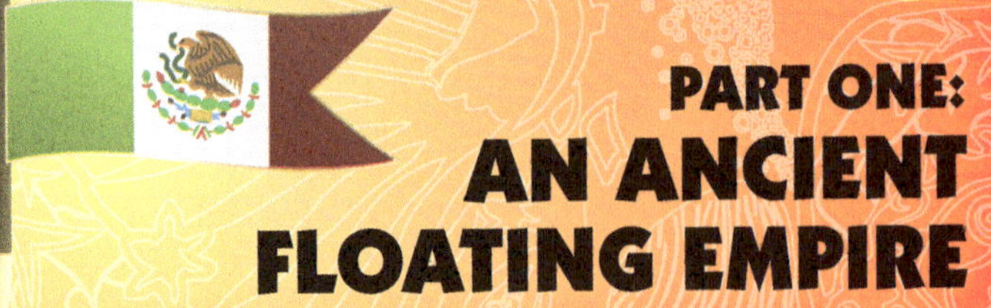

PART ONE: AN ANCIENT FLOATING EMPIRE

The Aztec Empire was an ancient Central American culture that is revered for its ingenuity in many areas of life, such as architecture, agriculture, engineering and empire building. The Aztec Empire, which thrived from the early 1400s, made its capital at Tenochtitlán (say *te-noch-tee-tlahn*), the site of modern-day Mexico City. Aztec legends relate how the early Aztecs saw a vision of a place where an eagle was perched on a cactus, eating a snake. They believed that, even though the land was a marshy lake, this was the place where they should build their city.

Today, the coat of arms of modern-day Mexico features an eagle eating a snake on top of a cactus.

Mexico's coat of arms

a seventeenth-century map of Tenochtitlán (left), drawn by Spanish conquistadors

The Kukulcán pyramid in Chichén Itzá (above) is among the most visited archaeological sites in Mexico

The **Amazing** Aztecs

People

Aztec (or "Mexica") is the collective name for communities that formed alliances throughout Central America between the fourteenth and sixteenth centuries. The Aztecs who lived on the island of Tenochtitlán were known as Tenochcas people. They were a subculture of the Aztecs who settled in the Valley of Mexico, on the island in Lake Texcoco.

Population

Before the arrival of the Spanish in 1519, the Aztec population in the Valley of Mexico was estimated to be over one million people. However, diseases brought by the Spanish, such as smallpox, may have contributed to the death, within three years, of up to 50 per cent of the population.

Period of Settlement

The Mexica settled in Mexico from the sixth to the sixteenth centuries. Alliances between different Mexica communities resulted in the formation of the Aztec Empire. Its first emperor, Itzcoatl, took power in 1428. For almost one hundred years from that time, the Aztec Empire grew and prospered until the Spanish conquistadors, led by Hernán Cortés, arrived in 1519. Cortés, who was welcomed at first, formed an alliance with rival communities to fight the Aztecs. Tenochtitlán fell to the Spanish and their allies in 1521. Faced with disease and war, the Aztec people went into decline.

CONQUISTADORS

Spanish conquistadors were armies of soldiers and explorers that conquered parts of Central and South America in the 1500s to increase the wealth and power of Spain.

a man dressed as a conquistador

Aztec **Ingenuity**

Architecture

The Aztecs built the city of Tenochtitlán using materials from abandoned cities. The city was divided into four equal areas leading to a twin-staircase pyramid, stone temples and a royal palace.

Agriculture

The Aztecs used sustainable methods to build self-contained islands on which they could grow a range of crops, capable of producing food all year round.

The Aztec City of Tenochtitlán

Reclaimed Land

Tenochtitlán was only about 14 square kilometres in area, but the city needed to house over 250 000 people. Land reclamation enabled the growing population to create small islands for settlement and for growing crops.

Engineering

Among the many examples of the Aztecs' engineering ingenuity were dams that filtered out drinkable water from Lake Texcoco's salty water, and aqueducts that channelled water from nearby springs to the settlements.

The Aztec Site Today

Mexico City is built on the site of the Aztec captital and, after land reclamation, the city is now about 1 500 square kilometres, with a population of around 19 million people.

2 Mexico's Floating Gardens

Chinampa is the Mexican name for a system of raised garden beds on small constructed islands in places like lakes, marshes and areas prone to flooding. These artificial islands are often called "floating islands", though they do not actually float. Xochimilco (say *so-chee-milko*), the name of the region where floating garden agriculture has existed for centuries, means "flower field".

a farmer tends to a maize crop, grown in chinampas

Tacos and Tortillas

The cave bean is an ancient variety of Aztec bean.

Aztecs grew maize, which is ground to make cornmeal.

Beans are central to making authentic tacos.

Cornmeal is used to make thin crispy tortillas.

Mexican waterways are used for transport, as well as agriculture.

Early History of the Floating Gardens

During the fourteenth century, the Aztec people needed a strategy to feed their growing population and large army. They drew on their knowledge of techniques from previous civilisations to construct the floating gardens to expand their land beyond their island city, and better manage their food and water, especially during periods of natural disaster.

Natural Disasters

In the middle of the fifteenth century, a period of natural disasters adversely affected the Aztec people and their crops, which resulted in years of famine. Once good rainfall resumed in 1455, the *chinampa* system became even more important to the survival of the Aztecs as they set about recovering from this debilitating set of events.

1446: a plague of locusts

1449: severe flooding

1450–1451: frosts and snow

1452: drought

1453–1454: famine

a locust

After the Natural Disasters

Following the natural disasters in the mid 1400s, the Aztecs embarked on an expansion of their floating garden system and worked out innovative ways to make them more productive. For example, they introduced a seed-germination program that ensured a steady supply of seedlings to grow and harvest food all year round. What made their ingenuity so remarkable was their ability to build a productive farming system in a seemingly uninhabitable environment.

Floating Gardens on Lake Texcoco

Lake Texcoco was a shallow basin made up of swampland. The Aztecs built *chinampas* in the shallow waters using natural materials from the surrounding environment. The basin was made up of five lakes, but after a flood, all the lakes merged into one.

LARGE GARDENS

Floating island gardens could be as long as 20 metres and as wide as four metres.

How the Aztecs **Built** a Floating Garden

Step 1

Use a long pole to probe down among the reeds into the lake bed to find a relatively stable base.

Step 2

Secure four long posts to stake out the rectangular garden.

Step 3

Build a fence in between each of the four posts by weaving together reeds and branches.

Step 4

Dig up mud from an area outside the four posts and collect vegetation like waterlily leaves.

Step 5

Layer the mud and the vegetation inside the staked-out rectangle and pile up the layers to about half a metre above the water level.

Step 6

Plant a willow tree sapling at each corner.

How the Aztecs' System of Floating Gardens and Canals Worked

TEXT TYPE
Explanation

Sustainable Ingenuity

The Valley of Mexico, where the Aztec civilisation existed during the fourteenth century, is prone to flooding. The lakes that form during floodtimes are generally shallow. However, the Aztec system of agriculture was based on making use of this geographical phenomenon to create a sustainable environment, even during periods of flood and famine. The Aztec solution was to build a series of canals and small islands, or *chinampas*, for the purpose of growing crops. The rectangular garden islands were able to produce enough food all year round to feed their growing population of several hundred thousand people. It would be relatively simple to build a similar system of canals and floating islands.

Constructing the *Chinampas*

First, long poles are needed to probe among the reeds in the shallow waters and down into the muddy lake bed, to find suitable places to build each of the *chinampas*.

Next, the *chinampas* are built by layering sludge from the lake bed and vegetation. This creates a natural compost to improve the productivity of the gardens. If the sludge contains animal and human waste, it can be drained into the lake.

WHY DIDN'T THE SEWAGE SLUDGE SMELL?

Scientists found a microbe in the sewage sludge at Lake Xochimilco that was a fast and effective aid to composting. The microbe produced no odour and prevented the kinds of germs and infections associated with raw sewage.

Chinampas and Canals

Once an island is sitting above the water level by about half a metre, a fence is woven around the mound using reeds and branches. The woven structure enables water to seep in. This keeps the soil moist and also carries nutrients from the lake bed sludge.

To strengthen the structure of the *chinampa*, willow trees are planted at the corners, enabling it to withstand periods of flooding. The intertwining root system of the willow trees grows quickly around the island garden structure and makes the *chinampa* strong enough to withstand erosion.

To provide easy access for the cultivation and harvesting of crops, a series of interconnecting canals is built between the *chinampas*. The *chinampas* can be accessed by boat.

Chinampas Survive Today

This system of *chinampas* and canals is still being productively farmed by *chinamperos* (or cultivators of *chinampas*) in the same tradition as their Aztec ancestors on Lake Xochimilco. Amazingly, Lake Xochimilco has survived centuries of drainage attempts in the Valley of Mexico, and provides a lasting reminder of this ingenious method of agriculture.

Chinampas Crops

Through their system of *chinampas* in Lake Texcoco, the Aztecs were able to support a population of over 200 000 people in the city of Tenochtitlán. Staple crops such as maize, beans, squash and chillis could all be grown locally. Fish and crayfish caught in Lake Texcoco supplemented a largely vegetarian diet.

4 An Aztec Chocolate Drink Recipe

Most Central American cultures grew and consumed cocoa, which is produced from the seeds of the cacao tree. The Aztecs boiled the seeds to make a drink they called *xocolātl* (say *sho-col-artl*), which means "bitter water". Instead of using sugar, the Aztecs added spices for flavour. Generally, only Aztec royalty and rich merchants consumed the drink. On hearing the Aztec word *xocolātl*, early European arrivals named the drink "chocolate".

Ingredients

125 grams semi-sweet chocolate

2 cups milk

¼ teaspoon cinnamon

1 teaspoon vanilla extract

Method

Step 1

Place chocolate pieces into a small, heat-resistant bowl big enough to rest on top of a saucepan half-filled with water.

Step 2

Put the bowl on top of the saucepan.

Step 3

Bring the water in the saucepan to boiling point and then turn down to a simmer to melt the chocolate pieces.

Step 4
Using a wooden spoon, stir the chocolate as it melts.

Step 5
Once the chocolate is smooth, turn off the stove element and use oven gloves to remove the bowl from the saucepan.

Step 6
Heat the milk in a pot, but keep an eye on it as it can heat up very quickly.

Step 7
Add the melted chocolate to the milk in the pot.

Step 8
Stir the melted chocolate and the milk until they are combined.

Step 9
Add cinnamon and vanilla extract to the chocolate milk mixture.

Step 10
Heat the mixture on a low temperature setting and whisk for two minutes.

Step 11
Pour the chocolate drink into a mug.

Step 12
Disfrutar! (Spanish for "Enjoy!")

5 Spanish Build a New "Floating" City

In 1521, an army of Spaniards and rival tribes of the Aztecs invaded and destroyed Tenochtitlán, the city at the heart of the Aztec Empire. In 1522, the Spaniards began their plans to build what is now Mexico City on the same site.

Mexico City Floods

Mexico City was built on the foundations of Tenochtitlán, and the problems of seasonal flooding continued, as they still do today. Despite the Spaniards' drainage systems and flood-control programs, the city was often underwater during the summer rainy seasons in the 1500s and 1600s.

present-day Mexico City

SPANISH ARMY LEADER

Hernán Cortés led the invasion and destruction of the Aztec Empire and initiated the construction of Mexico City.

Hernán Cortés

Water Drainage

Construction of canals in the 1700s provided some flood relief, but to this day, Mexico City's engineers continually battle the problem of water drainage during the rainy season. One of their main jobs is to maintain Mexico City's deep drainage system, which is a 68-kilometre tunnel up to 250 metres below the surface.

Drinkable Water

Unlike the Aztec city of Tenochtitlán, Mexico City hasn't been able to completely solve the problem of providing sufficient clean drinking water for its 19 million residents. Many wells have been drilled deep down into the aquifer under the city in the search for clean water, and this has caused the ground to subside. This has in turn weakened the effectiveness of Mexico City's drainage system.

AQUIFER

An aquifer is a layer of rock or soil from which water can be extracted.

As recently as 2009, severe flooding affected many residents of modern-day Mexico City.

6 Chinampas Survive Today

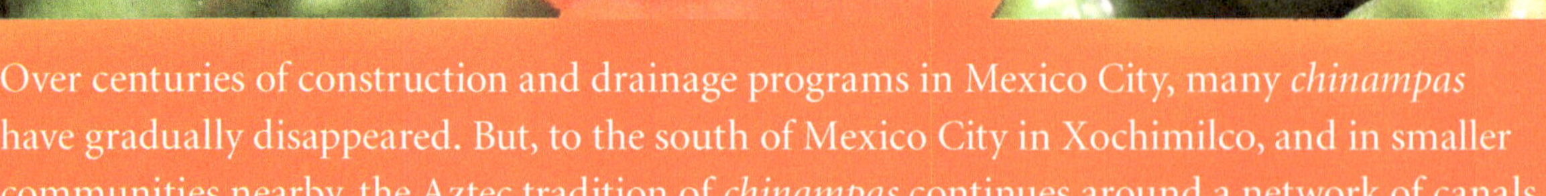

Over centuries of construction and drainage programs in Mexico City, many *chinampas* have gradually disappeared. But, to the south of Mexico City in Xochimilco, and in smaller communities nearby, the Aztec tradition of *chinampas* continues around a network of canals.

Chinampa Farmers

Mexican *chinampa* farmers are renowned for growing high yields of food crops and flowers using traditional methods on their fields at Xochimilco. But, in more recent years, environmental problems have caused *chinampa* farmers to make changes to their farming practices and their livelihoods. Some are listed below.

Chinampa challenge: industrial and residential waste

Many canal waterways have become contaminated, making them unsuitable for growing food crops.

Chinampa change: increase crops of flowers

flowers grown on chinampas

Chinampa challenge: unpredictable water supply

Climate changes and demands for water from urban developments mean water is not always plentiful.

Chinampa change: construct more irrigation canals

Chinampa challenge: growing urban settlement

Demand from an increasing population means high prices for land.

Chinampa change: sell land for housing

Philip Crossley, an American professor of geography, has studied chinampas *for many years. Here, he studies soil types in the* chinampas *region. After he collected small amounts of soil samples, the hole was filled in.*

Chinampa challenge: greater economic pressures

Rising prices and a weaker economy mean subsistence farming is no longer economical.

Chinampa change: grow fewer subsistence crops (e.g. corn and beans) and introduce a broader range of farming practices (e.g. farming animals)

a wide range of new cash crops are now grown in chinampas

Farming at Xochimilco

A farmer scrapes muck from the canal floor, which provides a fertile soil to enhance germination.

A farmer tends to a variety of crops, all at different growth stages.

Farmers dig irrigation canals to direct water from the main canals to other areas of the chinampas.

Several types of lettuces, in chinampas lined by willow trees, trimmed into a traditional shape.

For many families, canal boats are the main form of transportation.

Xochimilco on UNESCO World Heritage List

In 1987, Xochimilco was inscribed onto the UNESCO World Heritage List. The UNESCO World Heritage Centre has said of the chinampas farming system: "This half-natural, half-artificial landscape is now an 'ecological reserve'."

PART TWO: FLOATING COMMUNITIES

A History of Living on Water

Archaeological evidence shows that people have been living on or above water for at least 10 000 years. The remains of pole houses dating from this time, built over lakes or swamps, have been found in central and southern Europe. Ancient Polynesian cultures frequently built stilt houses over lagoons or lakes, and early African and South American cultures also built houses on poles over swampy or wet areas.

Sites for Floating Communities

There are several reasons for building communities in areas inundated with water. Choosing a site where there is adequate water for drinking, cooking and cleaning is important for all cultures, and building over a lake reduces the impact of drought or seasonal changes in rainfall.

Secondly, wet areas provide a good source of fresh food, such as fish, shellfish, birds and plants. Lakes and marshy areas also provide a reliable source of water for growing crops.

Thirdly, building over lakes and waterways provides a secure environment, making access difficult for predators and pests (such as carnivores and rodents) and also for human enemies.

a group of stilt houses in Tahiti, French Polynesia

Grand Canal, Venice, Italy

Centuries of Canal Boats

A History of Canals

Canals are artificial waterways built to enable vessels to move between natural rivers or lakes. As early as about 120 CE, the Romans started building canals in Great Britain to make travelling around the countryside easier. Canals became a safe, reliable and quick way to transport goods, livestock, crops and people from place to place, and over the following centuries, the network of canals around Great Britain grew.

The Industrial Revolution

With the arrival of the Industrial Revolution at the start of the nineteenth century, demand for reliable and quick transportation for the goods produced in Great Britain's factories grew rapidly. Advances in technology meant that canals could be built between lakes and rivers of different levels, and navigated using a series of water gates, called locks, that could raise or lower vessels in different sections of a canal.

Around 3 500 kilometres of interlinked canals enabled transportation almost everywhere around Great Britain. Many people chose to live, as well as work, on canal boats.

Canals became busy thoroughfares for transporting factory goods.

Tough Work for Canal Workers
1700s to 1800s

Before the Industrial Revolution, men usually worked on the canal boats and their families lived ashore. But as the railways became a cheaper and faster form of transportation, fewer goods were transported on the canal boats. As a result, canal workers' wages were reduced so much that it was more affordable for a whole family to live on a boat. Usually the women and children spent a good deal of their time steering the boat and caring for the horses that pulled the boats. It was a hard life, and families had to live in very cramped spaces to make way for the cargo on board.

Children on the Canals
1800s

Children living on the canal boats with their families often couldn't read or write, as they didn't attend regular school. Their main jobs were to lead the horse and open the locks. They often worked for more than 16 hours a day.

Laws were introduced in the 1870s to shorten children's working hours and improve their working conditions. Later, there were inspectors who checked that the children were going to school.

History

The Industrial Revolution

The Industrial Revolution was a significant period in history that began in Great Britain during the 1700s – an era when many inventions helped people to produce goods faster and on a larger scale than before. With the invention of steam-powered engines, people found many uses in manufacturing and transportation. For instance, steam trains made travel and transportation more time-efficient.

From Canals to Railways
mid 1800s

In the early 1800s, canal and railway transportation worked together, and in many places the railways were built alongside canal routes. The railways soon became the preferred method of transportation, however, as they were a faster option over longer distances, while canals were used for shorter trips.

9 Canals and Locks

Building a canal between two waterways at a similar level was relatively easy. A channel was simply dug to connect the two, and boats could navigate between the bodies of water with ease.

Canals on Different Levels

When joining two waterways at different levels – such as a mountain lake at a high altitude, and a lowland river at a low altitude – it was problematic. Water would simply rush downhill, making navigation downhill dangerous, and uphill impossible.

Locks Link Canals

This challenge was overcome by building a series of dams, or "locks", along the connecting channel. To enable a vessel to go uphill, a lock was sealed off and filled with water until it reached the level of the higher water further uphill. Then the uphill gate was opened and the boat simply moved forward to the next lock. To go downhill, the process was reversed, with each lock being drained instead of filled. The same system is used today.

The biggest locks in the UK can raise or lower vessels by up to six metres. The biggest locks in Europe can raise or lower vessels by up to 40 metres!

The UK

Water flows downstream to fill the first lock in a canal.

A ladder of locks raises the canal on a canal system in the UK.

The Grand Union Canal is a waterway with 160 locks and it flows for 217 kilometres between London and Birmingham in the UK. Here, boats travel along the Grand Union Canal in Warwickshire, UK.

Canada

The Rideau Canal in Ottawa, Canada, is a system of canals and locks that was opened in 1832, and is still operating today.

10 Floating Settlements in Asia

In many Asian countries, such as Thailand, Cambodia, Vietnam and Bangladesh, the wet season from May to October brings torrential rain. Millions of people in these countries suffer from some of the world's worst floods, which can cause loss of homes and lives, as well as outbreaks of disease and famine.

Aid agencies assist flood-affected communities, many of which are too poor to re-establish homes and essential services. Some cultures, however, have adapted to the rise and fall of rivers and lakes during the wet season by constructing floating communities with hospitals and schools. The novelty of floating buildings can even bring tourism to some regions!

BANGLADESH
VIETNAM
THAILAND
CAMBODIA

Tourism: Thailand's Floating Hotels

Millions of tourists holiday in Thailand each year. The picturesque River Kwai running through Kanchanaburi, Thailand, offers tourists many floating hotel experiences.

Settlement: Cambodia's Floating Villages

In the wet season, Cambodia's largest lake – Lake Boeung Tonle Sap – floods from heavy rains and the Mekong River's waters draining into it. The wet-season lake is home to a unique ecosystem of floating villages, houses on stilts, hundreds of fish species, and even crocodiles! Imagine having to cross crocodile-infested waters to visit your friends!

Commerce: Vietnam's Floating Fishing Villages

In Ha Long Bay, Vietnam, four floating fishing villages are well sheltered in coves from the effects of wet-season typhoons. The residents earn a good living from fishing and their floating homes are usually well built and comfortably furnished.

Education: Boat Schools in Bangladesh

When schools are flooded during the wet season, classes take place on library boats and school boats, providing students with classrooms and transportation.

11 Floating Homes in North America

Seattle's Floating Homes

In places like Lake Union, near Seattle, the USA, there is a long tradition of people living on permanently moored houseboats. Some are bolted to large, wooden poles, which can last for many years without suffering from wood rot.

Environmental Regulations

Dive inspectors need to check the undersides of houseboats regularly for wood rot and decay, often caused by organisms that chew away at the wood. There are environmental regulations associated with houseboat living, such as good waste management and sewerage systems. This is to ensure that the environment and amenity of the neighbouring houseboat residents are respected.

a houseboat in Seattle

Houseboats Near Portland

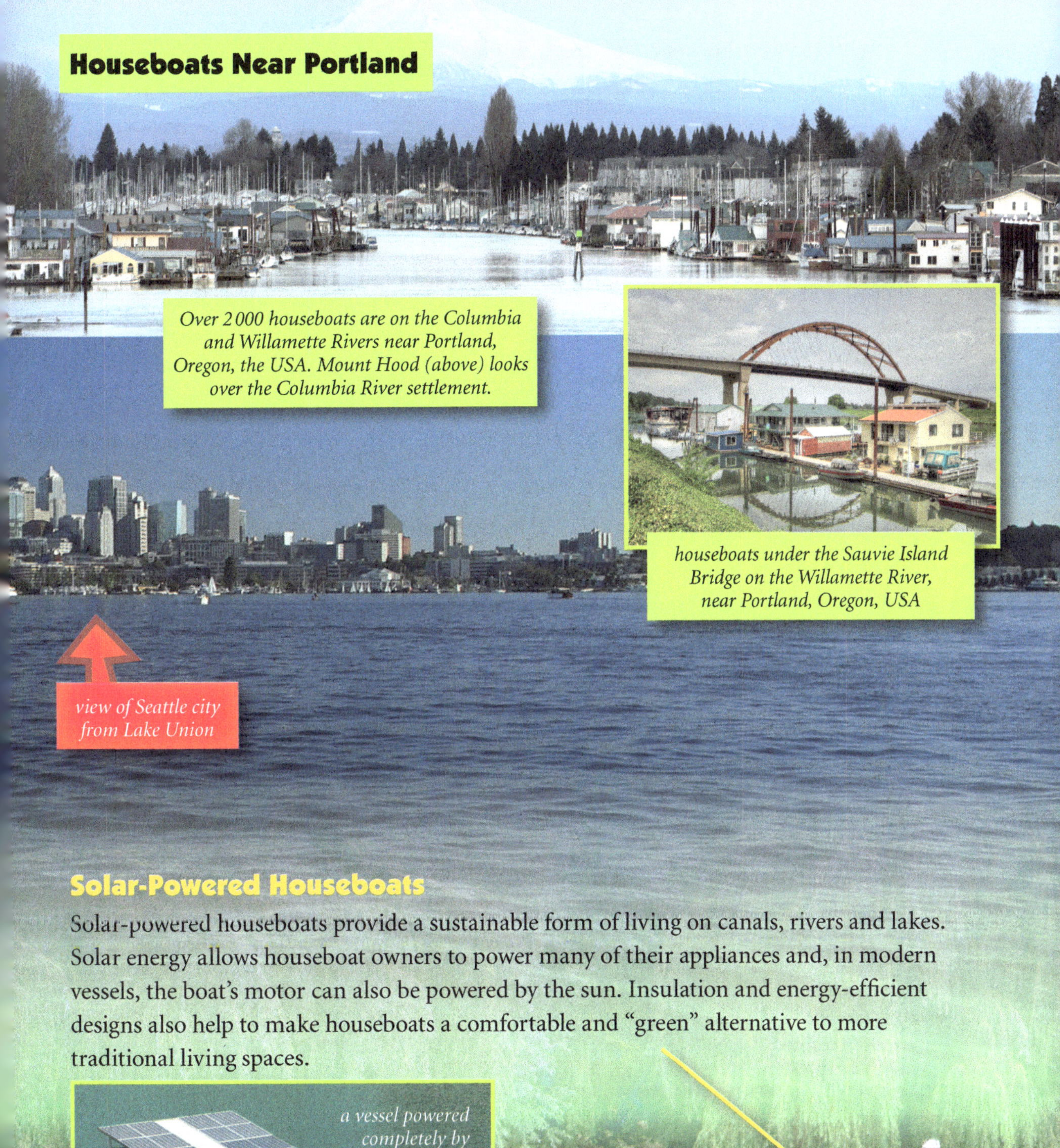

Over 2 000 houseboats are on the Columbia and Willamette Rivers near Portland, Oregon, the USA. Mount Hood (above) looks over the Columbia River settlement.

houseboats under the Sauvie Island Bridge on the Willamette River, near Portland, Oregon, USA

view of Seattle city from Lake Union

Solar-Powered Houseboats

Solar-powered houseboats provide a sustainable form of living on canals, rivers and lakes. Solar energy allows houseboat owners to power many of their appliances and, in modern vessels, the boat's motor can also be powered by the sun. Insulation and energy-efficient designs also help to make houseboats a comfortable and "green" alternative to more traditional living spaces.

a vessel powered completely by solar panels

12 Animals Afloat

Polar bears are well-adapted to life in the Arctic. Their ability to hunt and catch food in areas where the sea is frozen over for months at a time enables them to survive in the harshest of conditions.

Polar Bears Float on Ice Floes

Polar bears hibernate during the worst of winter, but in spring and summer, they need to catch large quantities of prey, such as seals, to replenish their energy and body condition. They do this by spending long amounts of time floating on large ice floes. In the past, these ice floes provided a stable platform for hunting and resting. As they floated over the Arctic Ocean, they also gave polar bears a large territory in which they could find food.

Climate Changes Affect Ice Floes

Unfortunately, changes in climate resulting from global warming have meant that ice floes are less substantial and melt more quickly than they used to. In turn, this has affected polar bears who are finding it increasingly difficult to hunt for food in the ocean.

Less Summer Sea Ice

Polar bears need sea ice to gain access to prey. This becomes a problem in summer, when the ice floes retreat from shore. During the warmer months the bears must either catch prey on land or in open water, which is very difficult for an animal as large as a bear. Many polar bears face starvation as they wait on land for the winter ice to form again.

Polar bears' powerful claws are thick, strong, curved and sharp to be able to hold onto the ice floes and haul out a seal weighing up to 90 kilograms.

Polar Bears Change Behaviour

Scientists have observed significant changes in polar bear behaviour as a result of environmental change. Before, polar bears would mostly consume seal blubber or fat to maintain their energy and body condition. Now, they are eating every part of the animal in an attempt to get as much nutrition as possible from every catch.

Threat for Polar Bears

If climate changes continue, and the ice floes become even less stable as hunting platforms, pressure on polar bear populations will become even more severe.

In 2008, the USA listed the polar bear as a threatened species under the Endangered Species Act. It is estimated that there are about 20 000 to 25 000 polar bears.

Furry feet have small bumps called "papillae" to prevent the bears from slipping on the ice.

a beaver in shallow water

a clear sign that beavers have bitten into a tree trunk to extract wood to build a dam

Dam Those Beavers

Beavers are mammals that make their homes by building dams in waterways such as streams, rivers and wetlands. Wherever they decide to build their dams, they will use whatever materials are around, and can destroy fences and parts of people's homes. They are considered pests in many states of the USA.

Index

Glossary

aquifer	A layer of rock or soil from which water can be extracted
Aztecs	The people of an ancient Central American culture known for ingenuity in architecture, agriculture, engineering and empire building
chinampa	A Mexican word for a system of raised garden beds on small constructed islands
conquistadors	Spanish soldiers and explorers that conquered countries in the 1500s to increase the wealth and power of Spain
floe	Floating ice formed in a large sheet on the surface of a body of water
houseboat	A boat designed and fitted for use as a dwelling
Industrial Revolution	The period during the 1700s and 1800s starting in Great Britain when many mechanical inventions helped to produce goods faster and on a larger scale
lock	A section of a waterway, such as a canal, which is closed off with gates and in which a vessel can be raised or lowered as the height of the water within the gates is raised or lowered.
UNESCO World Heritage List	A list of 962 properties around the world that the World Heritage Committee judges to have great cultural importance or natural value to the world
Xochimilco	An area in Mexico where floating garden agriculture has existed for centuries